AF481348

GRAVE GOODS

POEMS
BY CARDINAL COX

A BEATS! BALLADS!
BLANK VERSE! BOOK

BOOK 2

© Demain 2020

COPYRIGHT INFORMATION

Entire contents copyright © 2020 Cardinal Cox / Demain Publishing

Cover © 2020 Adrian Baldwin
First Published 2020

All rights reserved. No part of this publication may be reproduced, stored or transmitted in any form or by any means, electronic, mechanical, photocopying, recording, scanning or otherwise without written permission from the publisher. It is illegal to copy this book, post it to a website or distribute it by any other means without permission.

What follows is entirely a work of fiction. The names, characters and incidents portrayed in it are the work of the author's imagination. Any resemblance to actual persons, living or dead, events or localities is entirely co-incidental.

Cardinal Cox asserts the moral right to be identified as the author of this work in its totality.

Designations used by companies to distinguish their products are often claimed as trademarks. All brand names and product names used in this book and on its cover are trade names, service marks, trademarks and registered trademarks of their respective owners. The publishers and the book are not associated with any product or vendor mentioned in this book. None of the companies within the book have endorsed the book.

For further information, please visit:

WEB: www.demainpublishing.com
TWITTER: @DemainPubUk
FACEBOOK: Demain Publishing
INSTAGRAM: demainpublishing

DEMAIN PUBLISHING

<u>Short Sharp Shocks!</u>

Book 0: Dirty Paws - Dean M. Drinkel
Book 1: Patient K - Barbie Wilde
Book 2: The Stranger & The Ribbon – Tim Dry
Book 3: Asylum Of Shadows – Stephanie Ellis
Book 4: Monster Beach – Ritchie Valentine Smith
Book 5: Beasties & Other Stories – Martin Richmond
Book 6: Every Moon Atrocious – Emile-Louis Tomas Jouvet
Book 7: A Monster Met – Liz Tuckwell
Book 8: The Intruders & Other Stories – Jason D. Brawn
Book 9: The Other – David Youngquist
Book 10: Symphony Of Blood – Leah Crowley
Book 11: Shattered – Anthony Watson
Book 12: The Devil's Portion – Benedict J. Jones
Book 13: Cinders Of A Blind Man Who Could See – Kev Harrison
Book 14: Dulce Et Decorum Est – Dan Howarth
Book 15: Blood, Bears & Dolls – Allison Weir
Book 16: The Forest Is Hungry – Chris Stanley
Book 17: The Town That Feared Dusk – Calvin Demmer
Book 18: Night Of The Rider – Alyson Faye
Book 19: Isidora's Pawn – Erik Hofstatter
Book 20: Plain – D.T. Griffith
Book 21: Supermassive Black Mass – Matthew Davis
Book 22: Whispers Of The Sea (& Other Stories) – L. R. Bonehill
Book 23: Magic – Eric Nash
Book 24: The Plague – R.J. Meldrum
Book 25: Candy Corn – Kevin M. Folliard
Book 26: The Elixir – Lee Allen Howard

Murder! Mystery! Mayhem!

Maggie Of My Heart – Alyson Faye
The Funeral Birds – Paula R.C. Readman
Cursed – Paul M. Feeney

Beats! Ballads! Blank Verse!

Book 1: Echoes From An Expired Earth – Allen Ashley
Book 2: Grave Goods – Cardinal Cox
Book 3: From Long Ago – Paul Woodward
Book 4: Laws Of Discord – William Clunie

Anthologies

The Darkest Battlefield – Tales Of WW1/Horror

Horror Novellas

House Of Wrax – Raven Dane
A Quiet Apocalypse – Dave Jeffery
And Blood Did Fall – Chad A. Clark

General Fiction

Joe – Terry Grimwood
Finding Jericho – Dave Jeffery

Science Fiction Collections

Vistas – Chris Kelso

Horror Fiction Collections

Distant Frequencies – Frank Duffy
Where We Live – Tim Cooke
Night Voices – Paul Edwards & Frank Duffy

Dedicated to Dr. Gail-Nina Anderson, in gratitude, without whom, etc.

CONTENTS

MONSTER MOVIES

Parks convertible way at back

So doesn't obscure any view

Top down, he sits tall, feet on dash'

Bring bucket of 'corn on request

As sun goes down they run adverts

Trailers, a pair of old cartoons

They've all come for the main feature

Couples snuggle, guzzling cola

He though thinks, as celluloid spins

I knew him when he was a pup

I knew her before her first tooth

Knew it before atomic spill

Knew those before saucer landed

Knew him before formula found

Knew her when she waited tables

Knew them before acting lessons

I knew those before the scandal

Knew it before operation

Knew myself when the scars were fresh

SPONSORED BY THE BLOOD-MEAL FERTILIZER COMPANY

Thirty minutes broadcast late each Saturday night

This is not some New Deal arts presentation

Mid-west prairie homes tune to Radio Midnight

These are ghost stories to corner of the nation

Scriptwriters plunder literature for the plays

Classic tales are adapted for the small cast

Small-town farmers remembering Tolstoy for days

Depression, they said, but with wireless and pulps

Favourite productions taken out to school halls

In the low light they induce shivers and such gulps

Audience see faces of those they heard on air

Families gathered to tune-in, teachers in rooms

All listening as old chains rattle in a tomb

FAMILY SECRETS

Some stories are always best left unsaid

Do not question your food upon your plate

Nor ask what kept your mother up so late

Sometimes secrets are best kept by the dead

Paper don't lie; ink don't need to be true

Rumours and whispers are best never heard

Learn to ignore even the cruellest word

If you learned the truth what good would it
do?

Christmas time and wakes relatives gather

Look to aunts who might be quiet mothers

To escape is an expensive ticket

Backwash babbling brook of smallest blather

Eye uncles, as could be unspoken brothers

Family tree as ivy-clad thicket

THE WAKE

(1. v. cause to cease to sleep
(2. n. watch over a corpse and
attendant familial activities
(3. n. track left in a surface by a
passing body)

Room reserved under guise of a wake

Memories of departed ancestors toasted

Food and drink ignored as they huddle

Eldest are princes, nobles

Feudal lords whose rule is fear

Younger, more consensual, night-mayors

Clan loyalties mapped by sanguine
relationships

Families with un-births as bloody as any other

Youngest, still stretching, flexing

Trying to find their places

Haven't yet learned importance of tribe

Instead forge friendship web

In fires of abandoned factories

Waiting on tables, serfs tied to demesne

Thralls bound to masters

Here then is dark diplomacy

Treaties signed or broken

Becoming shepherds or wolves

SISTER HYDE

She's waiting for gas lamps to be lit

Anima in corset, gloves, stockings, dress

Instead of either/or, or sliding scale

Imagine Venn diagram – circles interlacing

Of biology, gender, orientation, nature,
nurture

Look to our simian siblings in their
bonobotopia

Whiptail lizards of New Mexico

Parthenogenic females entwined without
males

Fishes on coral reef swapping genders

To meet group needs for balance

Slugs and snails at heads and tails

Hermaphrodites in their mucus mess

Our flesh is destiny but flesh is malleable

(As ribofunk slogan once had it)

Be we hijras, katoeys or wraeththu

Her mirror still has makeup about it

She's waiting for gas lamps to be lit

TUPPENNY BLOOD, SHILLING SHOCKER

Human Tragedy! Ultimate Terror!

Read of Inquisition's infernal gaol

Suffer divine wrath or human error

Sensation! Horror beyond normal scale

Virgin daughters lost amongst savage tribe

Next week the new issue will be for sale

Misery recorded by starving scribe

Printed on latest steam rotary press

Buy each week or have library subscribe

Episode of Dick Turpin on Black Bess

The paper's rough but holds the midnight ink

Corsican bandits rip the maiden's dress

Cheap to have but, vicar says, worse than drink

More noxious to young than the city's stink

THREE SISTERS

In each of them is an eternal spark

Distant stars they cast forth their cool light

Catch the wind – spring through clouds – a
stringless kite

Dance a spirit beneath broad trees in park

Hair and make-up – secret sisterhood's mark

Summon mother muse with ancient rite

In each of them is an eternal spark

Distant stars they cast forth their cool light

Each embraced instead of running from dark

For they have called down the full-moon
bright

Theirs is a siren song we cannot fight

Drawing is the singing to which we hark

In each of them is an eternal spark

Distant stars they cast forth their cool light

UPIER

"Any baby born in caul or with teeth

And even if raised firm in true belief

Is doomed to wake within their cold grave

A thousand masses will not their soul save"

-        *Traditional Polish Rhyme*

The black-cross knights bring their Christ, cold

from coming so far from the south

with steel to the forest, fire to

the village, leaving graves as hoof-

prints as they travel, beheading

corpses before they can rise again.

Bishop in Krakow promises

only his faithful should taste his

God's blood, should wake again at some

point distant and leave the damp earth.

Dark woods, deep valleys hide secrets

other invaders come. We wait,

We wait for the lost, the alone.

Ravens watch while we count pebbles

PEACOCK GHAZAL

Wrapped in silk in night of darkness
She it is who offers bite of darkness

In cold mountains trees hold fruit
Between scuttles fox, a fright of darkness

Stars shimmer sharp in clear air
Silver knife glints light of darkness

Sweet peri in old ruined tower
Filled with strength, might of darkness

Lilith's granddaughter wears peacock cloak
Ebony eyes granted sight of darkness

CHRISTMAS WITH KING RICHARD III

Archbishop insists on leading service

Thin, sleepy choir sings mid-winter hymn

Somewhere in the river a pike slow swims

While small boys skate upon the moats
surface

Barons wait to see who's granted favours

Squires make start shining their liege's kit

In kitchen, twenty geese roast upon spit

A great pudding boils – filled with sweet
flavours

Mummers cavort outside a city inn

Five prisoners released into cold of day

Mistletoe beneath which maids may be kissed

Drunk thieves contemplate some seasonal sin

Hangman at rest in chair – no one to slay

Two nephews are off the king's present list

DEAD OF WINTER

She leaves bloody footsteps in the thin snow
The trail from the cooling corpse is clear
Copper thinks no detective needed here
Half-remembers once a tall, handsome beau

Now it feels that there is nowhere to go
Nervous servants recall the husband's sneer
She leaves bloody footsteps in the thin snow
The trail from the cooling corpse is clear

Bare black trees rattle in the east wind blow
The fatal weapon, they think, should be near
Frozen to her cold face, a single tear

There are some old secrets no one can hear
She leaves bloody footsteps in the thin snow
The trail from the cooling corpse is clear

WOTAN

Giants had been driven from the wholesome heartlands to fens, to mountains, to marshes and to ice fields. Those who would-be gods though were not content.

"We cannot create as giants did," they said, "and so these are not yet our homes. Even the dwarfs that delve and the elves of the edge make."

One of the brothers then said, "I will steal that which we need."

So Wotan the warrior, lover of women

To know secrets had knots tied, it was now

He hung on world-tree between heaven and hell

To pass the place where dead discover future and past

Body brought down, bloody and cold

Necromancer called, wizard wise in many ways

Brings back he who had gone beyond

The price though is a place at the feast, a bed
in the hall, an eye for their weakness. So
while Wotan named places, people and things
so that they might be, the wizard waited.

Ravens sit upon Wotan's throne-back. Wolves
hunch beneath the seat. He sleeps during the
day. At sundown the necromancer repeats his
spells – bloody are the sacrifices – places a
mead cup in Wotan's fist that stays undrunk.
While Tiwaz lead folk to war, it is his grey
brother who takes those that die to the
darklands to wait.

...AND HELL FOLLOWED WITH HIM.

-          Revelations 6:8

Revolution. War. Death crosses boarders

Horsemen in splendid dress ride hard through lands

Ignoring starving poor's imploring hands

Muttering that they must follow orders

Guillotine rocks upon cobbles, pooled blood

Into the void of chance slink foreign shades

They're hungry as ever for fresh French maids

And sniffing around grim battlefields mud

Darkest midnight, ancient feuds are settled

Territories flex, stretch forth and expand

So a new nobility arises

Tracks, once rutted become newly metalled

Vengeful commoners are now in command

Succumb to temptations of old vices

THEY FADE SO SOON

Suddenly like a sunset they are gone

Trees in autumn, they age, wither and fade

An old record that has been over played

Memory is there when the moon has shone

Humans scrabbling up the mountain to space

Or edge of an apocalyptic cliff

I've not got a crocodile's handkerchief

Oh they are such a sweet and tasty race

While we're the aliens they cannot see

Toyed with tyrants, superiority

Do they want a higher authority?

Maybe their future is our legacy?

You get used to them sleeping in your head

But don't attempt to understand their ways

You tell yourself that sometimes it's a phase

Then in a blink they are suddenly dead

A VERY ENGLISH DEVIL

Suburban Satanists start orgy with sherry

Amongst rosebushes – statue to Baphomet found

Meet at full-moon midnight upon the cricket ground

Divesting themselves of tweed as they get merry

Takes some bally Frenchman to frown upon their rites

To hire a darn exorcist against their worship

And, you know old chap, it really does take the pip

The nerve of him disturbing their midsummer nights

Doesn't he know we spent our youth at public school?

A bit of ritual spanking is nothing new

And if we must sacrifice some sweet chambermaid

Well you do have to follow each infernal rule

After dinner, in every beech-lined avenue

There are some who taste what other coves
have forbade

GENERAL PHERIDES SCHOOLDAYS

One thing I loved was the cross-country run

Out across the fields, away from class

Resting behind bare hedge, laying on grass

Often in numbing rain, seldom in sun

Father at embassy, so I at school

With pale boys who hated and I gave back

Though they learned fear when cold nights were black

Knew not to bully who they had named "ghoul"

Stupid masters detested for the pain

Exams I loathed for the jumble of ink

The cadet force perhaps was a refuge

So army offered me a chance to gain

Here was a place where I could at least think

But I've no love of bodies leaking rouge

MIRCALLA'S SWARMS

Now – workers are politicians – lawyers

Obtaining power in the sunlit life

Others – hippies – punks – rebels – never wife

Each woman possessed of strange dark auras

Drones were forces' men who married mothers

Spread German families to west and east

New cities – lands – new flesh on which to feast

None recognise sisterhood of others

Queens in the dark – each eternally young

Accepting tribute by daughters brought

Secret nests spread in so many places

Schloss Karnstein – Nineteen Forty-two – begun

Lebensborn hospital far from war fought

Maternity nurse careful – no traces

SEASIDE FORTUNE-TELLER'S SPREAD

First card – "The Twins" – shows choices in your past

Two roads and either you could have taken

A love or something – perhaps – forsaken

That opportunity was not your last

Next – "The Dancer" – who is in scarlet clothed

But drawn reversed to invert what it means

Does the gypsy desire to be queen?

Perhaps the loud adulation is loathed

One path – "Queen of Swords" – Boadicca the brave

A warrioress striving to be free

She who wishes to be fully obeyed

From the suit of Hearts we take "The She-Knave"

Crowned in bright blossom from the apple tree

Keeper of secrets otherwise forbade

MEANWHILE, IN NEW ZEALAND...

Nineteenth Century – colonists settle

Edge of the world – brought bones from
Bruges in bag

Revived the sharp one with blood, skin and
rag

Farmers learn to keep keen tools of metal

Maori recognise their tapu state

Come from Hine-nui-te-po's deep shadow land

That their existence is one that is banned

That these thin creatures bend natural fate

Despite light and noise – hunt only in town

Countryside confuses the pale ones

Some nights it's as though they fell off the
Earth

Sleeps deep in the cellar in rat-chewed gown

While the clear, broad sky is owned by the
sun

Remembers the damp flat land of his birth

LOCAL MUSEUM

Pipes brought from distant China

A famous stuffed mynah

Bird owned by Victoria Regina

In the dusty store of a local museum

Most of the bones of a mighty whale

Surcoat of crusader's mail

Rotten door of the town gaol

In the grimy store of a local museum

Postcards of historic views

Twenty-three pairs of curious shoes

An innovative sort of plough

Portrait of a prize-winning cow

A set of Bronze Age pots

Pistol that a highwayman shot

Salt chipped from the wife of Lot

In the higgledy-piggledy store of a local
museum

LOUHI'S SEVENTH DAUGHTER

First the fog curling between tombstones drift

She glides, skin as snow, hair reflects the
night

Waist thin within the fine-boned corset tight

She is aurora crowned Pohjola's gift

Coffee shop chats with bequiffed Jimmy Dean

Discussing darkness and void in the soul

Sometimes you find a mirror in the hole

He the doomed lively punk, she the dark
queen

Midnight L.A. TV she spins her rune

Upon a pile of human skulls her throne

Sisters include Maleficent Dracix

Cool and clear as a cloudless winter moon

High heels, black dress cleavage slash flesh
fast sewn

Handmaidens many a dominatrix

GOLF AT MIDNIGHT

Stiff fingers pushed into earth as a tee

Eyeball mounted upon flattened knuckle

No one here offers a grim chuckle

They know better than to get fidgety

Club has been adapted from a thighbone

The broad greens are quiet beneath the moon

This languid round has to be over soon

They are awaited by a loyal crone

Bunkers offer safety if play too long

Somewhere to dig in if sun comes early

While flags flutter in nocturnal breeze

On midnight course they are far from the throng

The loud neon city's hurly-burly

Hidden by silhouettes of distant trees

EX-GOVERNOR MAMUWALDE

"I may have the blood of African royalty in my veins, but I also have the blood of those descended from both slaves and slave-owners, the blood of criminals and cops, the blood of heroes and villains, of tyrants and liberators, of every race and every religion. I may have been an immigrant but I am an American..."

> \-   Prince Mamuwalde's speech on first
> becoming a city councillor

Governor has delivered his last speech

In limousine leaves senate of the state

Checks his antique watch to see if he's late

Only few knew his secret as a leach

Remembers being lawyer years ago

Later he was mayor of the city

And some of that slow rise wasn't pretty

What politician don't carry cargo

Brought peace and stability to the poor

Gave homes, work and some hope to those in
need

And it has all been hard work, not blind fate

He has watched young men go to and from
war

Again looks at his 'phone the text to read

"Would you consider being running mate?"

INVERTED CROSS

Puritan preachers, seeing devils in delight,

Attempt to combat the willing flesh of others

Just as would many grim missionary brothers

Who for native souls offer up a holy fight.

So in that which is alternate they see no good

And in themselves they find no single shade of
sin.

History though is written large by those who
win

Not by those who in others' shoes have ever
stood.

One tribe's demons are based upon another's
gods

Though the people themselves are little
different,

Their priests claim to know divine right from
hellish wrong.

And so hoping to even up eternal odds

I appeal to those few of us sapient

Suggest we should strive to be better than the throng.

THE WANDERER

The prophet said, "You will stay until I come back"

Thought little of that at that particular hour

And so I must wander along Earth's every track

In Spain lay for weeks upon Inquisition's rack

Avoided brave knights in their crusader tower

The prophet said, "You will stay until I come back"

Paris, saw guillotine where now there's a plaque

I watched blood flow, petals of a crimson flower

And so I must wander along Earth's every track

Deep in the bayou hid slaves in my simple shack

Cursed as more bigots arrived upon Mayflower

The prophet said, "You will stay until I come back"

With the hungriest man I learned to share my snack

Seldom saw good remain once those men gained power

And so I must wander along Earth's every track

Stood while holy priests swore my peoples' hearts were black

Alone remained standing in bleak Nazi shower

The prophet said, "You will stay until I come back"

And so I must wander along Earth's every track

ISCARIM

Corpse taken from tree, silver someone stole

Temple veil rent, earth shook, graves opened

He had hoped his death might make some amend

But his sins had forfeited his poor soul

Later, claws his way out of Potter's Field

Hungry, he searches through a moonless night

And he knows he must hide before first light

A curse that cannot ever be healed

He flits homeless about the Empire

Children carry his red hair as a sign

Three Xs mark their nocturnal feeding

One bloodline then amongst the vampires

A damned clan on living are forced to dine

Who must gather where others are bleeding

SPHINX CAFÉ

Old guys, outside café,

From their wicker chairs

Have seen them all –

English, French, Turks,

Arabs, Romans,

Greeks and Persians.

Skins Hollywood-dowager tight

Tanned to parchment –

Tubegrip round joints.

Sucking on shisha nipples

Of smouldering tana leaves,

Shabti staff totters

Bringing figs, bread, onions,

Hookah smoke cats curl, twist.

So they sit here dealing

Round Thoth's cards –

Watching beetle-pushed

Dung ball centuries pass –

Avoiding taking roads

To other lands.

ANGEL ROOF

On wooden-wings they soar, singing ancient
psalms

Carved across ceiling, gilded and guiltless

Witnesses to fen flood and thatch fires

Eternity at the level of eaves.

Survivors of Reformation and

Cromwell's Commonwealth Puritans,

While the worm that ate Jonah's shade

Trims wings, clips feathers

Spiders spin webs between heads and hands

Tallow smuts discolour paints.

Choir mouths carved open for centuries

Empty yet echoing bells, village band,

Organ and parish voices.

Yet they say, raise a ladder,

Be amongst them, back of one head

Will find a demonic mask.

Outside, gargoyles grimace

Here one who fell flies amidst

This host, warning always

To be on watch for evil's

Temptation amidst holiness

VAMPYRE TRAP

While hungry Lord Ruthven stalks the broad
boards

Threatening young maidens who have long
throats

Rapacious as the forests' hunting stoat.

Beneath their feet a contraption with cords,

Cog wheels, levers, sandbags, platform and
ropes

Waiting for the right moment to be sprung

As an alarm bell ready to be rung,

On this rough machine hang so many hopes.

Each castle proves to be a painted flat

Thunder rolls come from a drum in the wings

Even Pepper's Ghost is just angled glass

Upon a string flies the ominous bat

In this place they conjure magical things

But still we worry for the hunted lass.

REMNANTS OF A FOUND LOG

Low sky more grey than blue

Revenge – whale broke our ship

Icebergs heave into view

Lost sight of rest of crew

Below waves watched it slip

Low sky more grey than blue

Dreams of grass – damp with dew

Beards hold spray's frozen drip

Icebergs heave into view

No biscuits left to chew

Or water left to sip

Low sky more grey than blue

Not talk of lots we drew

Few words can pass our lip

Icebergs heave into view

One fate we always knew

Tear shirt to murderous strip

Low sky more grey than blue

Icebergs heave into view

IN THE MAGNETBURG FOOTHILLS

Georg, brave knight, died 1531

Tales were told of a great monstrous beast

Was buried by a good Catholic priest

His title passed on to son, on to son...

War hospital, 1673

A son, born to a displaced minister

Who earned a reputation sinister

Sought for arcane knowledge through alchemy

In an old book a square, "Lead, Load, Goad, Gold"

Creation never stopped, man perfected

Some do not want there to be no more poor

Some secrets though are not made to be told

Some aspirants are never selected

Ended poisoned, 1734

JESUS BLOOD NEVER SAVED

Rope rough

Round neck

Faces flash

Widows, sons

Fathers, mothers

Rubber glove

Fingers push

Girls met

Filter smells

Robbed men

Lever's clack

Own sweat

Forged letters

Acid dissolves

Fragile flesh

Jesus' blood

Never saved

Not real

If watched

Through glass

Signing cheque

Wounds pure

Film screen

Grail drip

Life penny

Arcade amusement

Gift washes

Sin away

Falling into

Jesus' arms

FR. AMBROSIO'S PSALTER

Pride? This is God given talent

They are God's words I preach through Lent

It is His spirit that fills me

Lord have mercy

Veiled wives sit in their hard pews

I become subject of their view

I'm merely a boat on His sea

Lord have mercy

Confession – whispered desires

Enflamed their sweet flesh perspires

A weaker man would swiftly flee

Please have mercy

Bold devils tempt at every turn

Mortal man needs wisdom to learn

But dark eyes twist unholy key

Mercy, mercy

Sanctity is armour enough

I shall call deep, hot Hades' bluff

And God's blessing shall keep me free

Lord show mercy

OTRANTO

Grim spectre stalks crusader walls

News is brought of chilling portents

Tapestries hang in draughty hall

Curse upon family's descent

Paintings release ancestral ghosts

Though few can guess what omens meant

Rumours of raiders along coast

Daughters – commodities of trade

In chapel priest observes the host

Down in crypt are heroes decayed

While lords maintain a heavy hand

Fealty has its debts unpaid

Serfs remain tied to barren land

Dissention, as always, is banned

MANY ARE DAMNED...FEW ARE SAVED

Flashman dandy drunk

In bar, pockets picked, tavern

Wench pawns his fob watch

Midnight B-movie

Hidden behind static screen

Monster hunts off-switch

Doctor Jekyll's glass

Tastes nice night before, next day

Fur upon the tongue

Shadow-wrapped daughter

Hiding from the taste of blood

Knife behind her back

Magic lantern show

The sleeper swallows the mouse

Time and time again

Alley, cartoon thug

Striped shirt and a billy club

Painting stars and birds

Green drink on fire

Steals back his father's brass watch

Flashman wobbles home

THE SONS OF GOD SAW THE DAUGHTERS OF MEN THAT THEY WERE FAIR; AND THEY TOOK THEM WIVES OF ALL WHICH THEY CHOSE.

- Genesis 6:2

In Babylon, ziggurats we cursed

Worshipped instead in sea cave

Sacrifices to clam-goddess Tiamat spawn

Flowers burnt upon midnight fires

Beast-men, men-beasts we abase ourselves to

In Rome, catacombs we rejected

Dead-god cultists sharing blood

Forests held our orgies

Garlands on lingam-stones

Beast-men, men-beasts danced with us

Children, learn what beasts you carry

Find totem-spirit, follow its path

Graffiti sigils in bus shelters

Arcane inscriptions on toilet walls

LE GRAND GUIGNOL

Puppets are back in their box at midnight

Dried blood between the theatre's threadbare
seats

Amongst Montmartre's dancers there is blight

Fell Qabbalists conduct a hellish rite

In pit the band seldom misses its beat

Puppets are back in their box at midnight

Backstage sits an old tub of face paint – white

Actress dreams of having a hotel suite

Amongst Montmartre's dancers there is blight

Cold alley and two lovers have a fight

Effects team perfect another grim feat

Puppets are back in their box at midnight

Something flies about Eiffel Tower's height

Draughty dressing room grate has lost its heat

Amongst Montmartre's dancers there is blight

Examine corpse for evidence of bite

Over cobbles thin cat hunts moonlit street

Puppets are back in their box at midnight

Amongst Montmartre's dancers there is blight

BLACK PILGRIMAGE

There are some places linked in peoples'
minds,

Tainted with legends of acts strange and wild,

Things threatened to the misbehaving child

And such sights as might turn a grown man
blind.

Yet some fell people search these places out

Plan and journey to the damnable spot

Where even a horse might refuse to trot

And the pilgrim must never harbour doubt

Brocken's high peak on April's final night

That righteous folk regard as rightly banned.

Noxious caves that spiral down to dark hells

Where few have witnessed some devilish rite.

Black basalt Chorazin in desert sand.

From beneath the sea comes the sound of
bells.

CONFUSION AMONGST THE STARS

Miss Edith must be beaten

She has been so naughty

She left her dinner uneaten

Miss Edith must be beaten

She wishes my mood would sweeten

But I must remain haughty

Miss Edith must be beaten

She has been so naughty

WALPOLE'S CAT

(After Thomas Gray 1716 – 1771)

I blame the glistering goldfish

Chubby and looking so delish'

In their old Chinese tub

Their languid mouths breaking surface

Watched by puss upon the bookcase

Horace out, at his club

Cat descends and circles the pot

Standing upon a shady spot

Tries to get its measure

Twice cat's length the vase is around

Cannot be nudged the cat has found

That still wants its pleasure

Front paws up it can now gaze in

Just so close to the tempting fin

Soon sits upon the lip

Whiskers twitch, shapes fill amber eyes

Tail flicks – unheard poor beast dies

Into waters it slips

OPHELIA'S GRAVE

Brazier to cast warmth and light

Thick canvas walls stand tall and blind

They have a hellish task this night

Their act is to be grim but kind.

Moths flutter into bowl of flames

Fragile wings singe and bodies fall

Love, not sacrifice, was the aim

Amongst trees unseen creatures call.

Sharp spades dig down into tight loam

Searching for particular prize

What they want's a singular tome.

Open the box, avert their eyes

One reaches down, he sees it there

Entwined amidst her mass of hair

DRAUGR

On the fell above the fjord

They say a miserly farmer

Who beat his wife too often

Died unmourned

Funeral rites forgotten

Improperly interred

Became barrow born

Frost forged

Dread Draugr

Cursed corpse

Blue bloated body

Odin's own

Hel-road highwayman

Wandering widow-maker

Plague purveyor

Insanities incubator

Madness' midwife

HALF-LIFE

He had half-watched armies trudge

Through crow dark forest before

Napoleonic infantry – Tsar's Cossacks

Now these boys – German officers

Local factory lads seduced

By cheep tales of easy hate

Dressed in second-hand seaweed green

Lightning bolts resting on collarbones

Half-hearted ideology of mastery

At night he took sentries

These half-fed soldiers tasting

Richer than stick starving peasants

Half-remembered his own enlistment

At the lips of a thirsty pale princess

Half-light left him careless

Surrounded – over powered – enchained

Officer gloats

"This one we keep

Gestapo can get their own

Radio lorry – we take him to Riese"

SNAGOV MONASTERY

Grim dictatorships becoming standard

In so many new nations

Archaeologist came to Orthodox monastery

Surveys medieval defences

Opens grave – the grave is empty

Ocean away Lugosi and Villarias

Channel a blood-drenched spirit

While dust of body blew away

Beyond Borgo Pass decades before

A dark flame fell to Hell

Of course the grave is empty

Four hundred years nuns brought flowers

When prison condemned preyed here

Abandoned, became villagers quarry

Empty grave's slab rubbed smooth

The grave is empty

Consecrated ground could not hold him

Scholomance eternals collected it

Leaving animal bones, pot shards

While they worked their alchemy

Empty grave

SWEET JUNGLE PHI

They say she comes as smoke

So the tales are spoke at night

Enchanting, so no fright,

Up nose, down throat so tight to lungs

Despite talisman bungs

Feasting upon the tongue, so choke

MISS JEKYLL'S CONGENIAL GUEST HOUSE

Guests are requested to refrain

From taking intoxicant drinks

Or prescribed tinctures of cocaine

No matter what your doctor thinks

Guests are all strictly forbidden

From entertaining visitors

In their rooms, open or hidden

I am quite the inquisitor

Guests must never, ever attempt

To hide bodies in house or grounds

No resident will be exempt

From questions if a corpse is found

Guests are all reminded that in

The unlikely event of fire

Don't blame it on an evil twin

Such things earn the management's ire

TANNHAUSEN: LOWER SILESIA

Blood transfusions fail – no heartbeat

Pinned as he is by wood, silver

Glass case exhibit moth.

Blood that is brought – thin, sickly

Whispers "Feed your sheep before

You drag them to slaughterhouse."

Those they take from are Russians,

Hungarians, Poles, Greeks, others

Knows when his slug fluid is given

To victims elsewhere in palace

Link is made – feels their fear

Deaths sicken, twist him

No elation of return.

White-coated gaunt lab technician

With aspirations perfects technique

Subject proves difficult to destroy

Not yet used to abilities

Impaled on stout stakes

Wielded by storm troopers

Thrown to incinerator.

Blood types matched

Volunteers picked

Mission for Fatherland.

VERGELTUNGSWAFFEN 4

West sky still draped dark blue hues

First stars out – they leave camp

At a run – heading for the lines

Every evening coming closer from east

First finding punishment battalions

Scum from gaols across Russia

Rifles pushed into hardened hands

Officers military malcontents

Choosing this over firing squads

Sometimes partisan peasants – eager

For glory days – to settle decade-old feuds

Then Red Army wolves descending

Upon brief bleak empire – grinding bones to

Gravel – waves reducing cliffs to sand

Torn flesh pink clouds behind enemy

Weary return – small victories

Next night – enemy closer still

AUTUMN HARVEST

They say she kept a nut

Hidden in a handkerchief

Little could she dream a glut

Of fruit beneath a strange leaf

Some fruit came out of Eden

Some from sunk Lyonesse

If you give the tales credence

These blooms phosphoresce

Moths gather at New Moon

Coated in toxic dust

These insects, dead so soon

Exhausted by nocturnal lust

Breath deep the heady scent

Chests swell to take it in

Then they stagger spent

Cold fire upon their skin

Pimples rise at each hair

Trembles wreck each limb

No longer lungs crave air

Now shy from sound of hymn

She sees one she knows

Stretching as languid cat

Dusk finds them drawn close

In only one seat sat

Autumn brings seeds on wind

Blown over vale and hill

Only one who has never sinned

Will look on this and think ill

FROM VENUS WITH LOVE

No one notices the spring shoots are strange

Bursting eager through the thin grey soil

Breaking forth from seed much-like a boil

Knowledge of alien weed might derange

First unfolding leaves attract no study

Tendrils spread and twist to catch and to hold

Here jobbing gardeners will not grow old

For the blooming plant's tastes are bloody

Flowers do not release the wandering bee

Birds too disappear amongst petals

Stray dogs about learn not to cock their legs

Poor creatures struggle but cannot break free

Trunk proves impervious to sharp metals

Botanists will surely learn to beg

BIOGRAPHY

Cardinal Cox has held such posts as being Poet-in-Residence of a Victorian cemetery (2005 - 2008) and of The Dracula Society (2015 - 2017). During the latter he was approached by a producer to create a one-man show High Stakes that he has toured including performances at Worldcon 75 (in Helsinki) and Dublin 2019: An Irish Worldcon. In 2019 he was included in Ellen Datlow's 'Worlds Best Horror' long list and had verse published in 'Shoreline of Infinity' and tribute collections to both R. Chetwynd-Hayes and Clark Ashton Smith.

ADRIAN BALDWIN (COVER ARTIST)

Adrian is a Mancunian now living and working in Wales. Back in the 1990s, he wrote for various TV shows/personalities: Smith & Jones, Clive Anderson, Brian Conley, Paul McKenna, Hale & Pace, Rory Bremner (and a few others). Wooo, get him! Since then, he has written three screenplays—one of which received generous financial backing from the Film Agency for Wales. Then along came the global recession which kicked the UK Film industry in the nuts. What a bummer! Not to be outdone, he turned to novel writing—which had always been his real dream—and, in particular, a genre he feels is often overlooked; a genre he has always been a fan of: Dark Comedy (sometimes referred to as Horror's weird cousin). *Barnacle Brat* (a dark comedy for grown-ups), his first novel won Indie Novel of the Year 2016 award; his second novel *Stanley Mccloud Must Die!* (more dark comedy for grown-ups) published in 2016 and his third: *The Snowman And The Scarecrow* (another dark comedy for grown-ups) published in 2018. Adrian Baldwin has also written and published a number of dark comedy short stories. He designs book covers too—not just for his own books but for a growing number of publishers. For more information on the award-winning author, check out: https://adrianbaldwin.info/

DEMAIN PUBLISHING

To keep up to-date on all news DEMAIN (including future submission calls and releases) you can follow us in a number of ways:

BLOG:
www.demainpublishingblog.weebly.com

TWITTER:
@DemainPubUk

FACEBOOK PAGE:
Demain Publishing

INSTAGRAM:
demainpublishing

www.ingramcontent.com/pod-product-compliance
Lightning Source LLC
Chambersburg PA
CBHW052106150726
48002CB00006B/2235